Blade of Light

Center for Basque Studies Basque
Literature Series, No.7

BASQUE LITERATURE SERIES

HARKAITZ CANO

Blade of Light

Translated from Basque by
Amaia Gabantxo

Basque Literature Series Editor
Mari Jose Olaziregi

Center for Basque Studies
University of Nevada, Reno

This book was published with generous financial support from the Basque Government.

Center for Basque Studies
Basque Literature Series, No. 7

Center for Basque Studies
University of Nevada, Reno
Reno, Nevada 89557
http://basque.unr.edu

Basque Literature Series Editor: Mari Jose Olaziregi

Series design © 2010 by Jose Luis Agote.
Cover design by J. L. Agote, with an illustration by Juan Azpeitia.

Library of Congress Cataloging-in-Publication Data

Cano, Harkaitz, 1975-
 [Belarraren ahoa. English]
 Blade of light / by Harkaitz Cano ; translated from Basque by
 Amaia Gabantxo. p. cm. -- (Basque literature series ; no. 7)
Summary: "Novel originally written in Basque that postulates
Hitler's victory in World War II and invasion of New York City"--
Provided by publisher.
ISBN 978-1-877802-95-9 (pbk.)
I. Gabantxo, Amaia. II. Title. III . Series.

PH5339.C36B4413 2010
899'.923--dc22

                                                              2010042530

Is there anyone who hasn't been hurt walking through tall grass sometime?

Grass can be treacherously sharp and cut like a blade.

And more. Who hasn't lain sweetly on the grass with a lover, wearing an increasingly rum- pled white shirt? Who hasn't brushed grass off trousers on the way down a hayloft, never stop- ping to think that life or just that joyous moment could end just then?

We lie on the ground and spy through blades of grass and, in that instant, the hero's statue seems vacuous, and the farmer's hunched figure as he cuts the grass, full of grace.

"What happened was that Russell Spencer, our artistic director, asked to meet because he had an idea for a gag about the origin of the Nazi salute.

"Russell's notion was the following: we needed to give Hynkel's character some background, we needed to make some sort of introduction. And this was one of the stories he proposed: in a little hamlet on the Braunau mountain, a spirited child straddles a staircase banister and slides down; suddenly he loses his balance, falls off and breaks a wrist. Immediately, the child's father—the head of the Brevesky family—decides that the way to make sure this never happens again is to raise the railing, then the child won't be able to reach it and use it as a slide. To this end, he sends his elder son (Hans Brevesky) to church first and the carpenter's next. While Hans visits the church, his job is to measure the angle of the railing of the tall staircase there, because his father wants his staircase to be exactly like it. But poor Hans doesn't know much about geometry so the only thing he can think to do is to measure the staircase's angle with his arm. So, he aligns his right arm to the banister, creating a 45-degree angle between the line of his shoulder and his head, and then, careful not to move his arm an inch, keeping the gesture intact, the arm lifted like that, he walks the distance to the carpenter's work- shop, to explain to the carpenter that his father wants him to alter the banister of the Brevesky staircase to match that exact angle... At the workshop on Grabenstrasse, a child plays with sawdust, draws houses of sawdust and blows them away. The child—young Hynkel—looks attentively at the boy Hans Brevesky with his upraised arm, and we realize that he is having an epiphany of the future, that this precisely is the moment the Nazi salute was born. Meanwhile, the carpenter, equidistant between the two boys, sketches out Mr. Brevesky's request on some old newspapers, smiling at young Hans's appearance while he assesses the angle of the boy's elevated arm, alternatively looking at his sketch and at the boy and back again.

"Russell wanted to insert those sequences as an introduction, or as a dream the dictator has—in a flashback, so to speak—and we did it like that in the first two drafts of the script, although we didn't film it in the end, it was too complicated. There are always two films, you know: the film that gets made and the one that gets lost along the way. The second one tends to be the better film, in almost every case. I have a feeling that the same hap- pens with historical events: there are several simultaneous possible paths, and we can only explore them with the imagination . . ."

—Charles Chaplin talking about filming *The Great Dictator* in a 1940 interview published in the *San Francisco Chronicle*

1

The boundless sea. How many times has he dreamed of crossing that boundless sea: cross it and, in the process, possess it. The fleet is made up of nine warships. They form three lines of three. The little man is aboard the middle one of the first three ships, clenching his jaw. He imagines for a moment that the force of his jaw guides the whole fleet: were he to point it slightly to the left, the three warships would veer left too, in response to his gesture. He often imagines objects inside other objects, and small worlds bound to bigger worlds by thin, knotted twine. He seldom laughs and when he does, his cheekbones take over his face, hiding his eyes until they are nothing but two slits. But not when he clenches his jaw, not then. Then the little man's eyes drink up the horizon.

Let us not get lost in a pointless guessing game. It is better to know it already. The little man's name is Adolf.

Adolf asks himself which was the most difficult moment of all in this war. The proclamation of the Vichy government, perhaps? A poisonous snake biting and killing that brute Charles de Gaulle just before the conference in Algiers was pure fluke. They had nothing to do with it; fate was simply on their side. Which was the hardest moment,

then, the most difficult one? Thwarting Marshall Patain's
hunger to govern alone, getting him to understand France
belonged to Germany and quieting him with a sonorous
title? Flattening the bunker in the center of London where
Churchill and his secretaries produced boring report after
boring report on typewriters with cushioned keypads, so as
to make no noise? Littering the beaches of Normandy with
mines just days before June 6, 1944? Infiltrating moles in the
French Resistance to ruin every single plan of insurgency?
Getting over the embarrassment of having to retreat from
Russia to regroup and attack again? No, none of that had
really been difficult. Some things have to be done because
it is prudent to do them: some objectives must be sacrificed
to pursue greater objectives with greater force. Even if it
was hard to swallow, the comedian had been his most difficult obstacle. Yes, that comedian had done a lot of harm,
there was no denying it. The film had opened in London in
1940 and given the allies wings. And what was worse: the
English continued to laugh at his expense for a long time
after that. Yes, but the time of easy laughs was over for the
English. They had little reason for laughter in the concentration camps of Wimbledon and Sheffield now.

He had lost sleep over the comedian, a lot of sleep. He
remembered perfectly the day Goebbels brought a copy of
the film to his office. He took the film out of its tin, placed it
on the projector and asked to be left alone.

"Are you sure you want to be alone, Mein Führer?"

He dismissed him with an angry wave of the hand: out.

He knew his subordinates had watched the film already,
behind his back. Instead of keeping themselves entertained
with *YANK* magazine during shifts, as was their altogether
forbidden habit, they had watched the comedian's film in

the bakery, projecting the images over a pile of sacks of flour. He knew it already. But Adolf could only withstand humiliation in solitude. Even though his men had already watched it, none of them would dare mention that strip of celluloid in front of him. He knew Eva wouldn't come into his office without permission, but he turned the lock all the same, just in case. In total darkness, he turned the projector on. The odious clown made him gag every time he repeated the words *Wiener Schnitzel* and *Kraut*. How dared he insult the German language like that! Yes, the comedian had been the most painful thing. Were some- one to measure the influence vanity and desire for revenge exert on the behavior of army commanders and leaders of masses of civilians, even nations, it would be revealed how relevant personal humiliations can be to the future destinies of peoples and countries. Yes, that comedian had been the most difficult thing.

But they dealt with him too.

And now, now they are crossing the Atlantic. He can hear the helixes of the Junker planes on the warships—taking off, touching down. Stukas, Messerschmitts, Focke-Wulfs. German planes. Erect Tiger cannons, made by Krupp; little round bombs hatched by I.G. Farben- Industrien nestled in the bellies of planes. He hears the ancient sound of swords crossing. It is sweet as music to his ears.

His boys are ready for the fight. And the little man is proud of his boys.

They are going to catch them all unawares. That is his intention, to take over the things that are inside other things, the smaller worlds inside the world, to become lord and puppet master of the twine and the strings that bind everything together, to grab hold of the reins of the world.

Adolf called his commanders to the strategy room. The operation was laid out on a map spread on an enormous table: the great swaths of territory under Nazi control marked by red string wound around hundreds of pins and, in a corner, visibly magnified, a separate map indicating all the access points and roads into Manhattan. The key to success was to take the Big Apple: once they were inside the city of skyscrapers the Americans would not dare bomb their own symbols and people. It would be easy. They had people inside too: more than twenty thousand North-American Nazi sympathizers had gathered in Madison Square Garden not long ago.

The comedian. That damn disgusting comedian. He had caused him the most pain.

"What you ask is very difficult, Mein Führer."

"We have invaded entire countries. What I ask involves just the one scrawny person. Not even that, he is half a person."

"But he's not just anybody, Mein . . ."

"I don't care how you do it. Just bring him to me." "It'll take some time . . ."

"Take as long as you need. Don't forget that we manufacture it now."

"What do we manufacture, Mein . . . ?"

Although the sea is calm, there is much movement on deck. They are preparing for an air raid. It is in the little man's plans that as soon as they approach the coastline American fighter planes will be sent out to attack in a desperate attempt to stop them from taking their shores. Seeing that work is progressing well he retires to his cabin for some rest. He puts Wagner on the gramophone but it sounds terrible.

"Scheiße! An orchestra, of course! I should have brought an orchestra along!"

Adolf hurries down the corridor that links his cabin to his lieutenants' as fast as dignity will allow. He climbs down the three steps that mark his rank, and the other three that serve his pride. He walks in without knocking. Herr Dieter is shaving and goes pale in seeing his Führer, feeling conscious of the fact that his Führer has never in his entire life seen him out of his uniform. Because uni- forms are like countries, disguises that hide us.

"Mein Führer! What is the problem?"

"An orchestra, of course!"

The way he says it, you would think that a gigantic octopus had come out of the water, wrapped itself around the hull of the ship and, playing a different instrument with each tentacle, impeded the ship's advance and deafened the entire crew with the ensuing cacophony.

"An orchestra, Mein Führer?"

"Yes, I want an orchestra. We can't just arrive like that, empty-handed, without music . . . music tames the beast and humanizes the human to the extreme! Ask the soldiers. There must be someone who can play something."

"But, Mein Führer, we're about to arrive . . . the American fighter planes could be here any minute . . ."

The little man returns to his cabin. He is thinking of the comedian. The repulsive Hynkel, playing with the globe. The barber of the ghetto, Hynkel's twin, who, at the end of the movie, usurped his place.

"It would be much easier to kill him with a telescopic shotgun . . ."

"No! How many times do I have to tell you that you must bring him to me? What do we have the Gestapo for?"

It wasn't easy but, in the end, they managed to capture that hateful impostor, that know-all comedian.

"And now, Mein Führer?"

"Now wait. Let him suffer a while."

"Should we apply the Marco Polo code to him?"

Marco Polo. He had been a traveler too, long before the little man. But he went about it differently. Yes, he was completely unlike him. Marco Polo collected small things: silk, exotic fruits, flowers and spices. He was happy with little, with gliding through places. With learning the languages and customs of faraway peoples. The little man, on the other hand, loves order. To anchor down, not to glide through. To finish the things, he starts. The pins stabbing the conquered countries and the red thread that links those pins mean something to him. A certain order, a sense of procedure, a delimited neatness. The little man can't stand holding a wrinkled newspaper . . . it repels him. Order and hygiene are absolutely essential to him, to maintain the order in his head.

Someone is knocking on his door. Two knocks, as agreed. Two: not insistent knocks that bother the peace of the person inside, and not weak ones that indicate a lack of vigor and personality in the person knocking. There is a certain intensity and cadence that is required to knock on a door. Not too ballsy and not too limp-wristed either. Not too much, not too little. That's how a door should be knocked on. He doesn't ask for much.

"Mein Führer? Dieter is asking what kind of orchestra you would like."

"Wagner. I want the orchestra to play Wagner."

2

The world is composed of strata. We each live in our corresponding layer, it is difficult to reach the one underneath or the one above. But sometimes it happens: on occasion, a man trapped under an avalanche digs a hole in the snow above him with the pointy end of his umbrella and finds himself in a strange world, to his surprise and the surprise of the people who help rescue him. The world, everything, is composed of strata. And for that reason, there are many things the little man doesn't know about.

First of all, he doesn't know the history of the crown of the Statue of Liberty. This statue was a gift from the French; it arrived in the United States, dismantled, on board the *Isère*, a sailing ship that took four weeks to reach the port of New York. There are engravings in the shipyard of Rouen that depict the process of splitting the statue into pieces and the difficulty of bringing it aboard the ship. The 225-ton statue was dismantled into three hundred different pieces, which were, in turn, placed inside two hundred boxes.

One of the port workers was Olivier Legrand. He worked down in the mines before becoming a stevedore, refilling mine drifts after the mineral was extracted. It was the worst job in the mines: refilling the holes others had made.

He packed the spaces where others had found gold or coal tight with earth so that excavation could continue farther below without fear of the galleries above collapsing onto the miners. It was a very important job, every- one agreed on that: if the drifts weren't thoroughly leveled dampness permeated them, and water could then filter down and ceilings cave in and collapse, putting the lives of the miners who were extracting metal in the lower galleries at great risk. But Olivier thought his job made no sense. "I undo what others did, that's my job," he used to say. He filled voids. He was a filler. Filling empty drifts with earth, as if burying invisible bodies—without prayer, without witnesses, without a vigil, without tears . . . that's what he did: he buried voids. "What I do isn't productive. If I were at least extracting metal," he used to think. Eventually Olivier grew sick of working in the mine and got a job at the port. He started on the cranes—or rather, under them—loading and unloading. That was a different story, he felt useful there. Now at least, the boxes he carried on his back weren't empty, even though he didn't always know what was inside them or where they were destined for.

The Statue of Liberty was beautiful. Even unassembled it was beautiful. Perhaps it was more beautiful unassembled, because often fragments surpass wholeness in their beauty. Often, empty homes are more beautiful than homes with people in them. Just like Turner's unfinished paintings are more beautiful for having being left unfinished. Or just like Picasso's *Guernica* was stronger and more beautiful before he finished it. Nothing can surpass the beauty of an unfinished work of art. No completed work can ever surpass the power and the beauty of a half-finished masterpiece. Liberty, once its pieces were assembled and the figure made whole, might be a disappointment.

Olivier was an orphan. He didn't have a wife. From the age of seventeen until the age of twenty-four he spent his life underground and, fearing he might spend eternity there unless he acted, he decided to find work at the port. But soon he was bored too. He wanted to go far away, go somewhere else. He had a crazy idea one day, while drinking *pastis* in a bar.

"Hey, Olivier, there is a blackbird nesting behind your ear."

"Hmm? What did you say?"

"Where are you? We have to return to the cranes. Time to eat up and go!"

Although it was winter they wore short sleeves, like they did in summer. Port workers in Rouen always dressed the same. Their arms were thick, and their hands calloused, enormous. Throwing small change onto the bar counter, Manu looked like he was spreading seeds for the sparrows. They left and went back to work.

"I just thought of something, Manu."

"What did the thrush whisper into your ear then?"

"You're working in the hold of the new ship now, aren't you?"

"Sure, I am, right under the skirts of the lady. If that's your concern you needn't worry: the girl is chaste."

Manuel half-laughed, half-roared. It was a port thing, the crass humor, the double entendres. The smelly armpits; the armpit breath, even. The armpit odor of the words they said. Women were far away. Farther, even, for Olivier. At least Manu had a wife who awaited him at home. And two hungry children hanging from her breasts, who would be old enough to be recruited when the Great War came along and would die on the front.

But things and worlds and lives are composed of strata, and he couldn't know all that yet.

"It's hollow inside, isn't it?"

"It's made of these thin metal sheets, yeah. But it weighs a hell of a lot, don't be fooled. Who knows what it will look like when all the pieces are put together."

"They say it's a woman with a raised arm. Holding a torch, I hear."

"That's a torch then! Yes, I think that's a single piece. They packed it on the back. The torch went in the backside! Ha ha!"

"I've heard there is a crown too?"

"That's a single piece as well. It's inside already. They couldn't fit that in any of the boxes. Hell it was difficult..."

"Don't complain so much. I'm still packing boxes of hake. I can't even feel my damn neck."

Olivier's neck hurt, it hurt a lot. He shifted boxes and more boxes. But this was better than filling up empty drifts. The fresh fish reached the port and it was his job to load it off boats and onto the carts. The fish were dead, but when he threw them onto the carts, he felt that as they fell amongst the ice and the salt they waved their tails at him, saying goodbye. Olivier lengthened the lives of the fish. As he shifted boxes from place to place, he felt like a sheep dog herding the fish, helping them take their first safe steps on dry land; like a nurse rushing to an emergency with a stretcher. He saved the lives of the fish and in the process saved people from dying of hunger. In the end, fish was a precious *mineral*, and now he was extracting it. These were the kind of crazy ideas that haunted Olivier's mind in the deep Rouen midwinter, as his neck froze over.

Olivier is a smart guy, he thinks of everything, and one
of the things he has thought about before tying up his knapsack is the softness of the things he has filled it with: he is
going to have to use his knapsack as a pillow and he doesn't
want anything hard inside it, anything solid or sharp. So,
he has left out his shaving brush, because its tortoiseshell
handle would be hard against his head and hurt when he
uses the knapsack as a pillow.

But pillows don't accommodate our shapes, our
heads adapt to the shape of our pillows. It is a mistake to
think that our bed accommodates our shape: instead, our
bodies end up resembling the beds we sleep on. Our abil-
ity to resemble furniture is something we must live with.
We each end up echoing a different piece, depending on
the movements, gestures and kindly and unkindly meant
laughter that, throughout our lives, shape our muscles—
facial and others.

Olivier has walked the distance from his home to the
port in the rain, in the dark. The streets, three hours earlier
than his habitual journey into work, seem different, more
complete, orderly, quieter... held together by a martial law
of obedience that the morning's hustle and bustle undo.
Packs of newspapers piled up, still bound with twine full
of possibility, like a deck before a card game, when the
cards still haven't been dealt and the deck is tight and perfectly aligned and no card juts out. One last look at the
streets he is leaving behind. Without nostalgia.

Just as if he were shoveling soil into a drift from which
others extracted iron.

The *Isère* is beautiful, an elegant ship. And it will look
even more so when they put the sails to the wind. It is nothing
like the fishing boats that bring the cold fish ashore.

He checks that the line that moors the ship to land is tight. It looks like it; it will hold his weight. His knapsack gets in the way. But he will manage. Holding onto the rope with his arms and legs, he climbs up the line and into the hold of the ship. It is a Monday, and he knows that the ship will depart this morning, early. He goes deeper into the belly of the ship without making a sound. He walks past the bigger pieces in the hold: box upon wooden box, all piled up, the dismantled woman, a gigantic book—God knows what lies between those unmanageable pages. He is enthralled by the crown lying outside the boxes—he can even see the hint of a face. Everything is hollow, it's true: as if ready to be filled with soil. Someone has already taken all the juice and metal from the lady. As if they had found Liberty under the earth and taken everything from her, emptied her, leaving only the shell.

"The girl is completely chaste! Completely chaste! Ha ha!"

Even smiles echo inside the hollow effigy.

Finally, he stands in front of the piece he thinks is best suited to sleeping needs: the rounded crown looks a bit like a cradle. The ship hasn't even sailed yet and his beard is already pushing through the skin. He can feel the coarse bush waking in his face. Olivier will miss spreading soap on his cheeks with the shaving brush, but his head will be grateful for the softness of the pillow.

He plumps up the softest part of his knapsack, places his temple on it and, inching his shoulder toward his face, curls into the fetal position. Soon Olivier sleeps.

3

A dark ship sails through dark waters. It is their last night before reaching shore. Someone is not sleeping. The someone who is not sleeping withholds someone else's sleep. Call it revenge.

"What was that painter's name?"

"Joan Miró?"

"No, the other one, the Spaniard."

"I think Joan Miró was a Spaniard, Mein Führer..."

"Pablo . . ."

"Pablo Picasso, sir?"

"Yes, that one . . . did you apply the Marco Polo code to him?"

"Yes, sir . . . His face ended up looking like one of his paintings. His most successful attempt at Cubist abstraction!"

"Thankfully we found out he was sketching that *Guernica* thing in time . . ."

"Yes, sir, and it didn't go beyond the sketch stage."

"You got rid of every pencil sketch, of course?"

"Most definitely . . . However, someone might have taken some photographs . . . one of his lovers . . . I think her name was Dora Maar, she was a painter too. We weren't able to locate those, not a single one. But at any rate, the painting was only in its initial stages when she took them."

"Excuses and more excuses . . . always excuse! Where is my orchestra?"

"On its way, Mein Führer. We are doing everything we can."

"Don't be stupid. I've told you a thousand times. We can do whatever we want!"

Propaganda. Everything can be achieved with propaganda, isn't that so, Goebbels? That was the secret to his conquering the whole of Europe. He spent much less than his advisers recommended on his army, but, by means of propaganda, made everyone believe they were four times as armed and prepared. It was paramount to organize a meeting between Goebbels and Henry Ford in New York as soon as they reached land.

The dark formation of nine warships advances, slicing the surface of the sea. Or are there six? Or maybe there are only three, and their engorged shadows.

4

The din in the port wakes Olivier up the following morning. The shouts of the machinists. The grunts of longshoremen, the grinding melodies of rusty pulleys, rusty cranes. He doesn't recognize any voices, but Manu must be there. He is leaving without saying goodbye. Manu might resent him for that. Good luck, Manu. If you can, don't send your children to the Great War. The knapsack has made a perfect mold of his head overnight: he has burrowed a big hole in it. He could refill his pillow with earth too. Even though he is far from the mines he still has a fixation with filling holes. The ship is about to set sail. He has spent the night curled up inside the head of Lady Liberty. It isn't all that comfortable. It is not comfortable to live inside the head of this woman. In fact, it is not very comfortable to live inside any woman's head. He should find a better place.

5

Adolf himself took care of applying the Marco Polo code to the comedian. When they brought him to that dark cellar in Berlin, the comedian no longer looked like the person who had appeared on screen. He was older, smaller, weaker, a lesser man. He didn't even have a moustache. Adolf hesitated for a second. Was that him? Yes, it was. And now he was in an equally dark and dank cellar, in the hold of the ship.

"Bring me a scalpel and get out of here."

The metal door was shut. The two men who had brought the comedian to the cellar disappeared simultaneously. There was a typewriter in the Room of Echoes. That typewriter didn't fulfill any function. The scalpels the little man held in his hands did. The comedian, how- ever, preferred to concentrate on the typewriter: q, w, e, r, t . . .; a, s, d, f, g . . .; q, w, e, r, t . . .; a, s, d, f, g.

"What about some Wiener Schnitzel for dinner, mister comedian?

The comedian was frightened, but he looked Adolf in the eye.

"So, I'm the Great Dictator, then. And I'm tossing the

globe in the air, is that right? "Charles Chaplin proudly presents: *The Great Dictator . . .*" That's how you advertised the film, is that right?"

The comedian preferred to stare at the typewriter: asdfg.

"Is that right?" Qwerty. Asdfgh.

"Now. Maybe it is time to swap places. Let's see. "The Great Dictator proudly presents: Marco Polo and the comedian in the Room of Echoes." Do you know why they call this cellar "The Room of Echoes"? Why do you think? Do you know how they made people see sense in Marco Polo's time?"

Let us stick with the term *little man*, to fully imbibe the soothing effect of words, as if words were penicillin, as if words had analgesic power. Let us spread words like they used to spread morphine in the camps, generously. Let us continue calling him *little man* and let us leave *Adolf* aside for now—that first name is discomforting. We will continue referring to him as the little man, then: and so, the little man takes the scalpel in his hand and checks it under the lamp, and the scalpel's sharp blade glints under the light. That blade of light is an escape route from the present, a tunnel, a crevice that has just opened up, thinks the comedian. I wish I could enter through that pathway of light, through that thin blade of sun-drenched grass that is the scalpel.

But the comedian is tied to a chair, barefoot, and   his toenails just then start to foresee the bleak future that awaits them.

There is no silent cinema in the dark cellar. No silent films in the Room of Echoes. *The Great Dictator* was the comedian's first sound film. The Great Dictator. Amid howls of pain, the comedian shouted *Wiener Schnitzel* or *Kraut*—those were the words on his mind and in his throat. A hand holds a white handkerchief: not the comedians hand. It's the little man's hand, he uses it to pat the sweat off his forehead. One corner of the white handkerchief is red with blood.

But since the handkerchief is folded in four, if a corner is red with blood, in fact four corners are red with blood. The same would happen with a book too, if one corner were stained with blood all the pages in that corner would be stained. Stained with blood? Does blood stain? Or does it wet, or color, or quench thirst . . .

Of blood.

A handkerchief and a book. Both similar, both balms. The white-paged book and the immaculate handkerchief. Stained with red, wet, colored, a drinking trough for beasts to soak up words from. After Adolf's men—yes, let us call him Adolf now—applied the Marco Polo code to Pablo Picasso his *Guernica* was never finished, but the comedian finishes it now, with his neck stretched, howling.

Here ends the era of silent cinema.

Shouting *Wiener Schnitzel* and *Kraut*. *Wiener Schnitzel* and *Kraut*. *Wiener Schnitzel* and *Kraut* . . .

The typewriter remains there. But doesn't say anything. Yet it contains all words.

6

When will we reach port, Lady Liberty, my concubine, my darling? I am a prisoner of this ship. Imprisoned inside the Statue of Liberty, herself a prisoner of this ship. I am a stowaway. Liberty's stowaway. And who doesn't carry a stowaway inside? Who isn't a stowaway, thinks Olivier. Those who don't have a stowaway's soul don't deserve to live. Is there anyone who doesn't carry a void they need to fill inside? Manu, where are you now? Do you think of me, Manu? Who will fill up the little hole I made in your head. The *pastis* and *demi-de-bière* we used to drink at the port, who will you drink them with now? The job Olivier used to carry out underground, who does that in people's heads? Whose job is it, to fill up the holes left in our heads by memories, misfortunes, sudden deaths and unfair, untimely life lessons? Who fills those drifts up with earth so that water won't filter through and cause the galleries in our brains to collapse and bury our reasoning, the little sanity we have?

He would write to Manu when he arrived in America.

His neck hurt and he kept stretching it up and down, to relax the muscles. Just like you, Lady Liberty, said

Olivier to the curved metal hosting him. My neck wants to be free too. He thought the pain in his neck was worse for sleeping in that uncomfortable, make-do cradle, than it had been for carrying boxes and boxes of hake. It seemed that way.

He had a feeling that the slight hump on his back grew a little every day too.

The ship swayed a lot, she rocked violently to one side and the other all the time. He vomited inside the crown, everything he had, down to the bile. Olivier was embarrassed. Lady Liberty was looking at him. That was all she did. Look. She was impassive. But Olivier wasn't. He was adrift inside that crown that swayed like a cradle. And every time he threw up he tried to think up a noble motive for it, something nobler than silly seasickness at any rate, something more important, like love or fever or home- land, something that forced him to be inside that crown and made him throw up like that. But what homeland, what fever, what love…?

Nausea permeated everything.

7

"The comedian is really unwell, Mein Führer. He's been throwing up for two days. He can't keep anything down."

"Well deserved. He has eaten too many Wiener Schnitzel."

"Too many Wiener Schnitzel, sir?"

Dieter didn't understand it. It was a perverse irony, which could have been more perverse had the little man seen more of the comedian's films. He could have said, for example: "So he's throwing up? Give him the sole of a shoe and a bit of salt, it will settle his stomach." But to be ironic like that it is necessary to be cultured. Oh, cultured, such an ugly word. No, forget it. Let us erase it. Let us say enlightened. In order to live, it is necessary to be enlightened. We need light to live, we need big windows. The greatest punishment of jail is windowlessness. Irony requires windows. Ah. That's it. Yes, that's better. Irony requires windows. The comedian goes to a porthole, tries to open his mouth, it feels like his jawbone is broken. His cheeks and eyes look unreal in the reflection the little window returns to him, too round and bruised. His eyes are wide open, and stretching his neck upward, it is almost as if he were completing the *Guernica*. True, some paintings can be completed only like that, in a dark ship's hold, in a rubbish dump, amid much blood, unbeknownst to the painter. While he sits in a Paris café smoking a pipe with his legs crossed at the ankles, someone completes the painting he left unfinished.

The ships approach the American coastline at a steady pace, but the comedian can't know this because all he sees is water and more water through the little porthole, which isn't sufficiently big to encourage his irony. It is impossible for him to know where they are headed, which prison they are taking him to and what those waters, which to him are just water, are called. If he had pockets, he wouldn't take his fingernail-less hands out of them for the remainder of the journey. But his prison uniform doesn't have pockets. Shoe laces, belts and pockets are forbidden to prisoners. He might hide in a pocket. Hide from the world, who wouldn't? Or he could use the pocket as a bag to asphyxiate himself with. The pocket is a tunnel, an escape route. Or don't things inexplicably disappear from pockets? And what's even scarier: don't things that don't belong to us inexplicably appear in our pockets sometimes, like keys, foreign coins, dead lighters, rings, strange and mysterious things, not ours?

And we don't know what to do with those things that aren't ours, what locks those keys might open. The thought of it frightens us.

"Right now, my hands look like a miner's hands," the comedian thinks, and he starts to cry, he cries from the core of his heart, more fully and profoundly than when the little man applied the Marco Polo code to him; he cries longer, and louder. Afterward he feels proud of his miner's hands.

I am no longer a comedian. I will never laugh again. Never ever. Never with witnesses.

Not far from him, in the belly of the ship, the little man feels a cloud of regret, a small one: that this ship of steel doesn't have a mast or sails. That would be something else. He would like to have a man atop the mast, like those seventeenth-century expeditions did, a man in charge of shouting "Land ho! Land ho!" But he was born in the age of steel and this has made him of steel. He is not like Marco Polo, who was happy to collect spices, silk, exotic flowers and other nonsense. He is Adolf. Hynkel, Heinkel... Let us keep calling him *the little man* for now, and think that words can be a balm still.

8

Many years before, in the hold of another ship, Olivier suffered immeasurably, as if expressing his sympathy to the tortured comedian sixty years in advance. He and his knapsack were thrown here, there, everywhere; like a blind man without a stick, he couldn't keep his balance. Sometimes we express solidarity without knowing that we are doing it, toward people we don't know, toward heroes of eras different from our own, toward some who haven't yet been born and others long dead, toward those who will be born many years hence and will die when their time comes. Olivier curled up inside a crown in the middle of a storm. Olivier with his back undone. The sea applied the Marco Polo code to him. He did have a noble motive for every time he puked inside Liberty's crown: unintentionally, he expressed his solidarity, support and sympathy for the comedian.

He saw the coastline after four weeks.

He stretched and descended from the crown that had been his cradle for that time. When they brought the merchandise to land, what would they think about the dry vomit inside of Lady Liberty's head? He accidentally kicked a rat sleeping on top of the gigantic book. What lies inside liberty? Rats and vomit, that's what, my friends. He brought the knapsack down from the crown. In a few hours they would reach port. Before nightfall he would set foot on land, and start looking for work in New York.

It was June 17, 1886.

9

"We've had problems with comedians before. Did you know Robert Hughes Lambert? I'm sure you did, all of you comedians know each other. We caught this guy in a queer bar and deported him to Drancy. Why are there so many queers among comedians? No answer, I see. Are your nails sore still? This Lambert guy, I remember, was about to bring out a movie. All that was missing was the soundtrack. The film director asked permission to come to the concentration camp and record the sections that required Lambert's voice from the other side of the fence, imagine. They came to ask if I would allow it, if I gave my permission . . . of course I did! I love cinema, I said, I love Greta Garbo, I love those Bengal tigers of the celluloid, let them record whatever they need, let them tie the microphones to the barbed wire . . . see? I too have done something for the history of cinema . . .

The comedian spoke for the first time. He couldn't help it.

"What happened to Robert?"

"I don't know. I don't think he ever left Drancy. The film came out, that I know for sure. I think the title was *Mermoz*, unless I'm mistaken. But let's forget all that. Do you know where we're going?"

10

New York was nothing like he had imagined. It was much more beautiful than he had envisaged. The green fields of Central Park, the incessant bustle of the port. But above all, the stone buildings. A whole world lived inside that island. He found a job as a stevedore again and, with his first wages, apart from buying a shaving brush, he rented a room south of the island, near the docks.

"Name?"

"Olivier Legrand."

"I'll give you room 114."

Unbelievable. Room 114. There were only three floors and twelve rooms in the hostel, yet room numbers started at 111. Clearly, the grandiose air of the city impregnated everything.

He could see the docks from room 114. Day by day, from his window, he watched as they assembled the sheets that made up Lady Liberty, as the pieces interlocked and embraced each other, growing into the structure imagined by Eiffel. The day they finally put the crown on her head he couldn't help but feel a bit overwhelmed. "My bed, my cradle… now it holds that woman's dreams," he thought. Vomit and rats. He thought it unlikely that he would ever do anything remotely as important. He could die in peace.

And yet, he met a woman before he died, and he married her. Marie Ann.

He didn't quite die but, as the years wore on, he had to visit the doctor more and more often. It didn't take him long to realize that things weren't that different either side of the ocean. He thought of Manu sometimes, of the *demi-de-bières* they used to drink in the port's canteen. He never wrote to him.

Olivier's back was getting more and more bent. How bent? Let us say that it resembled the handle of the comedian's walking stick. Quite badly bent, indeed. People often made fun of him because of it. His wife Marie Ann's massages and rubs eased the pain, but he looked worse by the day.

"You've carried too many boxes of fish!"

"Time to retire already!"

"This guy is French . . . maybe he worked in Nôtre Dame, hand in hand with another hunchback I know . . . Ha ha ha!"

President Grover Cleveland officially unveiled the statue on October 28, 1886. The sculpture was conceived by Frédéric Auguste Bartholdi, and he dedicated twenty- one years of his life to the project. At first, he used his mother as a model. But his mother grew old and tired of standing up, and, in the end, he had to ask the maid to take his mother's place. And as a result, Frédéric Auguste Bartholdi fell in love with the maid and married her.

So, Liberty was made to the image of a maid. It is a beautiful paradox, for those who like to collect paradoxes.

There was an old rumor that said that once, while visiting Rouen, Bartholdi saw a woman stepping out of a curtained carriage with rumpled skirts and hair undone and loose around her shoulders, and that the vision of that

woman wrapped in a lace mantilla made such an impres-
sion that inspired the sensual features of Lady Liberty. But
there is no way of confirming it; it would be too much of
a coincidence for Bartholdi and Emma Bovary's paths to
have crossed like that.

Marie Ann, Olivier's wife, got pregnant twice, but lost
both children. This didn't help Olivier's hump much. As
well as having to carry the world on his shoulders, he
was condemned to carry the souls of his two unborn children too. He was grateful for Marie Ann's strength and the
solidity of their love and friendship. Marie Ann was everything to him. If, when day turns to night, our thoughts
turn to a certain person, that's the surest way to know we
really love them. And Olivier didn't need sensuous horse
drawn carriages with luxurious curtains to find love: he
had no doubt that Marie Ann was the woman of his life.
He met her in Central Park, in the middle of a downpour.
Everyone ran in search of cover, only Marie Ann didn't.
That was why they walked down the path together. Olivier
couldn't have run if he wanted, not with his hump.

"Do you enjoy getting rained on?"

"No, but I really dislike rushing. We all make choices in
this life."

To choose to meander. In this life.

A gesture she made to dry her hair made him fall in love
with her there and then. That's how things happen. Quite
simply. We see a gesture and think to ourselves, this is it, here
I stay, to live inside this gesture, there's a beam of light here, a
gleam like one from a scalpel or a blade placed under a lamp.
Who knows where that gesture might take me, where the
path of light this gesture invites me to follow leads. That
is love. That and the thought that turns to someone as day

turns to night, drawn by horse or on foot, but to them, as if pulled by a magnetic north.

Meanwhile, many people took Lady Liberty as a symbol of freedom. But no one in that city knew—not even Bartholdi himself, the man who had lain naked with his maid and in the process learned to love her gestures—that what had once been Olivier Legrand's bed now watched over that lady's dreams.

It had to happen sometime. He couldn't hold it anymore: one day Olivier exploded.

"I came to this damn country inside the crown of the Statue of Liberty, you imbeciles! That's why I have this hump on my back! Have some respect, for God's sake!"

His confession only encouraged the laughter and mockery of his colleagues. Olivier felt a great emptiness inside, an emptiness he knew would have to fill up with earth before his spirit collapsed onto the tiny miners he carried inside.

11

The Normandy one wasn't a real landing. What they were
about to do on the docks of Manhattan, that would
be a landing. On the horizon, the little man begins to see
the staggered line of skyscrapers on the southern shore
of Manhattan, the uninterrupted irregular line of a comb
erects like a proud tuft of grass, buildings like ears of wheat,
alignments of suspicious reeds with shadows that fall into
the water. When he sees the Statue of Liberty with her arm
raised he feels she is giving him the Roman salute.

Adolf swells with pride. He raises his arm too, looking
at the statue.

"She's one of our own, Dieter!"

"She was a present from the French to the Americans,
Mein Führer."

"Are you sure?"

"Yes, Mein Führer."

"Bah! The Frenchies. A weak people, a cowardly sub-
species. But we won't destroy it . . . yet."

He found no resistance. Nine ships. Fighter planes. A
fleet. First Europe, now the world! Long platforms slip out
toward the port, like tongues. Tanks lead the way. On foot,

German soldiers march quickly, rifles in hand. The people at the port are in shock, the newspaper seller can't believe what he's seeing . . . How can something that I am not shouting about be happening in this city? It is I who sing the headlines! I create them; all scandals, all shocking news are colored by my voice . . . But this isn't in the evening news, it isn't . . . And just then the city's newspaper boys in their distinctive braces and caps start shouting without newspapers under their arms, or holding newspapers now destined to wrap fish; they start improvising the headlines of not-yet-born newspapers, right there, making history the way it should be made, coloring the events with their voices, making them news.

"Newsflash! Newsflash! The Nazis have taken Manhattan!"

They shout it once or twice, until a loud bang from one of the rifles out-thunders the voices.

Adolf is amused. The orchestra has started playing one of Wagner's pieces. Sorry, *piece* is not a word that can be applied to Wagner. We are talking about an entire machinery. There aren't enough instruments to play Wagner in the orchestra improvised for the occasion. Or in the whole world. The instruments that will best interpret his staves are yet to be invented. That is the only thing the little man finds a bit disappointing. The instruments that can express his worldview haven't yet been invented.

The comedian goes to the porthole. He realizes they have arrived in Manhattan. He can't believe his eyes. There are Nazi flags and swastikas everywhere, armed soldiers swarm the port, like flies crowding the bloody entrails of an eviscerated dog. People are being cornered, detained, they are trying to escape through the chaos and commotion.

Two officers unroll a sheet of barbed wire, God knows
what they are going to fence in. When he realizes that they
are using the barbed wire to round up about a dozen people
he can't help shutting his eyes before the barbed wire
squeezes them. His elbow hurts.

"I must thank my elbow," thinks the comedian with
miner's hands. I have to be thankful that it has taken on
all the tiredness and the pain; thanks to my elbow I no
longer think of my lost nails or my broken ribs, my purple
eye, which looks like a rotten pear, the way boxers' eyes do
when they lose fights and cry in darkened gyms. There are
occasions, such as this one, when the elbow takes responsi-
bility, takes charge, deals with it all: thank you, elbow.

"But it isn't just that, the elbow is talking to me," he
thinks. The elbow has a life of its own, the elbow wants to
tell me something. The comedian stands up with great difficulty. He tries to break the porthole glass with his elbow.
Once, twice, three bangs. Only a small crack appears in
the glass. But his elbow still hurts. The pain is immense. A
silent howl. And this means that the elbow still calls him,
that it is begging him to continue. And the comedian hits
the porthole with his elbow again and again, ignoring the
orders from his brain and following only the elbow's, until
he breaks the glass. Cold air floods his cell, and with it come
screams, the sounds of people trying to escape, and shots.
Strange sounds. Sounds that don't belong in   a city, in a
port. The sounds of war, maybe. He has tried to remove
all the shards of glass from the porthole, his hands are
bleeding. The hole is too small for a person to get through.
But he isn't a person anymore and this is an advantage in
the circumstances. His shoulders hardly fit into the hole.
He has to push one shoulder through first; his arms get in

the way, useless things. One last crack from his neck and
he is out. He falls out. One shoe stays inside his cell, but
he is outside, falling to the water, spreading his arms: but
for now, as he plunges head first into the filthy waters of
Manhattan's docks, having the use of his arms is really of
no use.

12

The landing caught Olivier Legrand near Wall Street. He knew the Nazis had conquered all of Europe, but he would never have dreamed they would dare attempt the same across the Atlantic. Neither he nor anyone else. "They wouldn't dare," President Roosevelt had just said. But if the most criminal minds dared carry out the craziest ideas, then what? No one knows what to do, no one is prepared for the situation. That would require them to be as crazy as the perpetrators.

Olivier was an old man by then. He was almost ninety years old and had walked with a stoop for a long time, and liked going to Battery Park, cane in hand, to watch the sunset. He liked sitting in profile to check that, every passing day, the bend of his hump was in more perfect alignment with the angle of Lady Liberty's crown. This eased his mind. No, he hadn't done anything more important in his life, it would be hard to find anything that surpassed being a stowaway inside Lady Liberty's crown, being her minder in her journey across the Atlantic. And now this. Germans. The Nazis, lords of America.

He sees terror swirl in the eyes of a child playing with a spinning top. Women and children run in every direction. There is a rabbi on the ground, his face and beard lying in a pool of blood. Lady Liberty stands there, a silent witness. Gripping his cane tightly, Olivier walks toward Brooklyn Bridge as quickly as he can. No one notices him. For a while he thinks he must be dead, he must be a ghost, a wandering soul. But even though he looks everywhere, he can't find his corpse. So, he decides to keep walking.

Then his eyes find him. By Dock 19. A man with a single shoe on, getting out of the filthy water, his face and hands black with congealed blood, all of him coated in an oily reddish film of filthy port water. He looks like a reptile, a regressive reptile that never made the leap toward the next evolutionary stage of amphibian-human; a reptile who, millions of years behind the rest, decides to climb that last step and become a mammal. It is never too late.

His face feels vaguely familiar, the face of this stowaway; Olivier thinks that maybe the familiarity stems from his shipwrecked air, not so much from his face. He can hardly stand up, he limps, practically drags his body along. When the man notices Olivier staring at him, he stares back at his cane, mesmerized, as if he, the stowaway, knew Olivier too. Olivier senses that this half-man half-reptile has seen the world begin and end before his eyes. The stowaway comes up to him, almost crawls over, tries to stand up, grabs his shirt. But he keels over: suddenly he is on the ground. Then he raises himself up again, with difficulty, and puts his hand on Olivier's cane. And with that everything falls into place: the moment he touches the cane the fog lifts from Olivier's brain. The cane tells him who the man in front of him is: the comedian, the very famous comedian! He has seen his movies; he remembers the one about the immigrant who arrives in New York in search of a better life particularly well. And the one where he helps an orphaned boy. It is a reptilian, orphaned immigrant he sees in front of him right now. Human and inhuman. He helps him stand up and together they head home, step by step, down a narrow side street the invading troops kindly haven't occupied yet.

13

Olivier couldn't believe it. It was a miracle. A signal. A gift that a God he didn't believe in had sent him. Inside the belly of the beast had come the comedian, laughter, joy, the only possible salvation. Newspapers had announced his disappearance a long time ago. They took him for dead. United Artists had even published his obituary in one of the newspapers with the greatest circulation. That very year they had honored his career at the Oscars.

The comedian was very weak. He spent seven days in bed in Olivier's Lower East Side home. He couldn't even sit up. The first four days his stomach would only accept only broth. Olivier, with renewed strength, fed it to him with an old spoon. That young man was closer to death than Olivier and somehow this made his own death seem further away.

Olivier's wife lay on the other bed, still as marble, struck by a paralyzing sickness. She could hardly open her eyes. Olivier wondered if his wife sensed anything. Did she notice that there were two mouths for him to spoon feed now? That in their room, on the bed next to hers, was the man who had made the films they had not so long ago watched together on a cinema screen in Broadway.

Olivier caresses his dear Marie Ann's white hair. Unable to move, the comedian observes the tender scene between husband and wife. Where is he? What nightmare is this? Where has cruel fate brought him? What is happening out there? So many thoughts crowd his mind the comedian can't say a word. He has returned to the age of silent cinema. He suspects the man who rescued him in the port when he was practically dead knows who he is, and feels grateful he has never praised him or told him how great his movies are. He is grateful for his discretion, for the special care with which he tends to him, care he knows the old man would extend just as tenderly and discretely to any other half-reptilian orphan who emerged from the dirty port waters. He suffers watching the invalid, immobile woman on the bed next to his, and senses there are no other rooms in that house. He can't remember if they walked down a corridor when they got there, how many doors they opened and closed, he was barely conscious. But he suspects there isn't much more than that room to the house, and concludes that Olivier must sleep on the floor in the next room—although he doesn't know Olivier's name yet. And what can I do now, he thinks, what can a comedian do; the war is lost, there is no more laughter, nothing else to laugh about, other than death, but that's pointless. Death has no windows.

Marie Ann, the comedian and Olivier. Olivier wonders who among them will die first. If it is he, what would happen to the other two? This worries him. What would the comedian and Marie Ann do if they were left on their own? What then?

The radio announces there have been searches in nearby homes. They are looking for something or someone. They are looking for someone, a thing, a bad thing, an evil thing, a thing turned reptile, a thing devoid of human essence. They are always looking for something or someone. They compile a new census, change the names of the streets, make blacklists and unmake them, erase old words, substitute old lettering with gothic writing. They change the pages of history, clean them up, de-rust them. Where is the U.S. Navy? Where is President Roosevelt? The radio is silent again, only classical music plays every now and then. Wagner. They are no mere pieces, they are an entire machinery.

The city is a Wagner phone: Wagnerberg.

14

"So similar and yet so different, the steam rising from a cup of coffee and the smoke rising from a just-fired shotgun, don't you think?"

The comedian smiles, for the first time.

It is the first day he manages to leave the bed and, although he doesn't say a word, he thanks Olivier with his eyes all the time.

"You know, I came to this country in the hold of a ship. You won't believe me but I came inside the crown of the Statue of Liberty. I hid there. It was a long time ago, in 1886."

"Why wouldn't I believe you?"

Those were the comedian's first words. Bring a box lined with silk, something soft, to hold these words worth gold; bring the receptacle of essences, Marco Polo, bring those first words the comedian uttered to the Great khan! Olivier the hunchback, the same Olivier his colleagues laughed at for years: retire already, man, you've carried way too many boxes of frozen fish, no wonder your neck is frozen too! You've carried too many boxes, man, that's your problem, and isn't this the guy who worked hand in hand with that other hunchback in Nôtre Dame? And now: why wouldn't I believe you. Those words. A balm. He felt his neck stretch and his head lift. He felt proud hearing those words.

The comedian took Olivier's hands in his. His were even more wrinkled than Olivier's: most fingers were missing the fingernails. Those little crusts of dried blood reminded Olivier of anthracite, of the color of the soil he used to fill up drifts with.

15

The little man knew what he was doing. He had housed the interim government in the Woolworth building, and filled its top ten floors with all the pregnant women from Harlem and the Upper East Side, and every child under three. That did away with the possibility of air raids on their headquarters. He punished Dieter by having him guard the top floors. He deserved it; after all, it was his fault the comedian had escaped. He could count himself lucky not to have ended up in front of a firing squad. In truth he had done pretty well putting together the orchestra and the little man was in a forgiving mood. Things so far had been easy. Seamless.

For months now, the megaphone systems newly installed in the streets of New York played only Wagner. Charlie Parker, Dizzy Gillespie and all the 52nd Street jazz musicians were made to play Wagner dressed in white suits, sporting swastikas in their arms, live from Radio City Music Hall.

Within a month they had taken the East Coast, including the White House, of course. The little man discarded the possibility of taking his government to Washington;

his advisors said it was too risky. It was safer to stay in New York, in the Woolworth building.

And where were Franklin D. Roosevelt and his cohorts? The president and his team had escaped to the

West Coast and were sheltering in Los Angeles. The little man's army would take some time to get there. But they were the makers of time, they needn't hurry.

The little man wasn't very interested in desertic Los Angeles. Only in one rather renowned neighborhood there, the one they called *the dream factory*, the one nerve center left out of his control. The only weapon that President Roosevelt and his team had left to fight him with. Propaganda. This frightened him a little. Just a little.

Had he strangled the comedian when he had the chance he would feel calmer about it all.

16

"You don't happen to have a typewriter, do you?"

The comedian smoked a pipe filled with the dregs of tobacco Olivier got him. It wasn't pipe tobacco but he smoked it in a pipe all the same.

"No, but I can get one."

"I could go out to get it. I think its time I did something, don't you think? I'm fine now."

"No, you can't. You can't leave this bedroom. It's still too dangerous."

The comedian shows his frustration with an impatient gesture. Olivier thinks of describing what he witnessed at the bakery that morning: a soldier pushed the head of a black baker into a sack of flour until he choked to death. But he doesn't. Instead, he tries to ease his mind.

"I'll bring you a typewriter tomorrow. I know where to find one."

Olivier goes out. Ever since the occupation he walks very slowly, cane in hand. Even more slowly than usual. He seeks the sympathy of the German soldiers. Poor old man. But he is full of pride, feels strong as an oak, capable of walking without his cane even. He has a mission now.

To find a typewriter.

First, he gets the food. His ration card allows him food for only two people, the tins of tuna come from the black market. When he asks for a typewriter they look at him with suspicion.

"A typewriter? Now?"

As if he had asked for some out-of-season fruit.

"What do you want it for?"

He wants to shout "to change history." To hold the reins of our lives and our world again. But he doesn't.

"I don't know . . . a hand-written will doesn't seem appropriate, don't you think?"

He takes a grimy, twice-folded piece of paper from his pocket.

The boy at the counter, who has a mole on his cheek, stares at him with surprise, then goes to the boss and says something. The boss peeks out from behind the beaded curtain with a look of mistrust on his face. Olivier knew the place—now a musty ill-lit bazaar selling anything to anyone—back in the day when it was an illegal gambling den.

Only when his boss gives the nod does the boy take a dusty typewriter out of a cupboard. It looks very heavy.

"This is quite expensive. How much cash do you have?"

"Does it have a ribbon?"

"Yes, but only one. We don't have a replacement."

"I'll take it."

"Seven fifty."

"I thought this joint wasn't in the business of fleecing people anymore."

"Excuse me?"

"Forget it . . . I'll give you seven, no more."

"It's very heavy, I don't know if you'll be able to carry it."

"I will, don't worry. Hang on . . ."

Olivier sits on a chair. The boy with the mole on his cheek looks on—what's the old man doing?

"Put it on my back."

The boy glances at his boss as if asking what to do. The boss signals to get it over with. So, what if this crazy old man wants to write a will and maybe kill himself afterward, or before, so let him, carrying that typewriter on his back is certainly suicidal. All that for a will: a white sheet of paper and a dead man with an Underwood on his back, a snail and his shell. Rest in peace. But no, it isn't resting that this old man seeks.

"Don't worry. I'm used to it. I worked as a stevedore in the port."

Later the boy with the mole on his cheek notices the folded piece of paper the old man forgot on the counter. It is not a grimy, handwritten will, but an old newspaper cutout.

A typewriter advances very slowly, like a tortoise through the streets of Manhattan. Tortoises could change the world if only we let them.

17

The comedian spends weeks typing away at the type- writer. He writes by the window, from early in the morning, next to Marie Ann. He hardly lifts his eyes from the machine, only to look out into the light. It makes Olivier think that whatever the comedian writes flies out of the window directly, that every time he turns the roller the just-finished line doesn't just land on the page but flutters away toward the glass; all those lines, everything he writes, a beautiful song . . . and not at all what Olivier told the boy in the shop, an old man's will. Or perhaps it is the opposite: maybe the comedian writes what he sees in that square of light, automatically, as if he were just receiving dictation. His eyes swing from the window to the page. Light feeds what the comedian writes, and what he writes is light, a spark of hope. It is as if every page he wrote were a receptacle of light and he just the harvester. In those days of darkness, he collects all the light, whatever little there is, and weaves it together, gives it shape. He makes an inventory of light at the darkest of times.

It is one way to fight.

Olivier went into the room only twice a day: to feed Marie Ann and caress her hair and leave a tray of food on the comedian's bed first, and to collect the empty tray later. The bed hadn't been slept on for days, it remained untouched. The comedian fell asleep on the typewriter whenever he was tired, resting his fingertips on any letters—actually, not any letters but very well chosen ones, the precise ones to help him continue where he had left things, like, for example Z- and y-k-l-o-n-B, or maybe s-o-t-h-e-n, and he would sleep like that, with his fingertips on the letters that would remind him where to continue when morning came.

He couldn't write at night because the Nazis cut the electricity supply as soon as night fell, every night, all over the island. Throughout the whole island bar the Woolworth building, of course. The light was always on in there and, at night, the hum of a printing press filled the air.

"Why do they cut the electricity supply every night?"
"Because they need it for the printing press in the Woolworth building."

"But why?"

"Because they are printing propaganda."

"And what does the Nazi propaganda say? What are they promising now?"

"That they are going to improve the electricity supply."

The joke had played in the ears of every Manhattanite.

But the comedian was not in the mood for light-heartedness. Some days he didn't even touch his food. Olivier didn't say anything when that happened. Not one word. Light harvesters must be left to gather and weave their light ray by ray at their own pace, in their own way, without anyone's interference.

Olivier listened to the comedian writing from the other side of the door: the sound of the keys was a sign that the world was still turning. It was a light factory, that, a factory weaving a cloth of light and lighter and then multiplying the light by a hundred. A giant patchwork of light for the world. Light that would cover the world like a circus big top made of pure light—and all thanks to a typewriter. A typewriter he had carried on his hump. Olivier was proud of that. He had thought that he had accomplished the most important thing in his life a long time ago, as a stowaway inside Liberty's crown; he didn't think that anymore. He knew that what he was doing now was the most important accomplishment of his life.

On occasion, quite seldom, the comedian had days of doubt. Crouched against the door, worried, Olivier followed the scraping noises the comedian's chair made on the wooden floor. On days like those the keys were silent, the light factory was quiet. And the days and the hours passed so very slowly when the comedian didn't write. So slowly. For Olivier, they were eternal. Luckily such crises never lasted long. Every time, just as Olivier was ready to give up; as, with his ear glued to the door he sensed the comedian's will waning, the keyboard started singing again, the comedian started thumping at the keys with renewed energy. Ever since the radio played only Wagner's music, the typewriter had become his radio: the rhythmic hammering of the keys, the roller's swishing caress of the pages, the little ding that marked the end of each line, the sure, competent tug that signaled the completed page . . . it was a whole new Morse code. And it spoke about a stack of pages that grew and grew.

It seemed to him that Marie Ann was happier too.

That she was smiling in her own way; there was an imperceptible but sure change on her quiet face.

18

"Everything is going as planned, Mein Führer, we've got the 52nd street musicians building the mausoleum."

"Have you heard from Fritz Lang?" "I hear he's gone to Hollywood too."

The little man furrowed his brow and wrinkled his nose. When he saw Fritz Lang's *Metropolis* he thought he had found, stamped on that roll of celluloid, the signature of the man who could create the ultimate propaganda film for the Third Reich. But Fritz Lang rejected his offer. Fortunately he was able to count on Leni Riefenstahl.

"And the comedian?"

"We are looking for him but we can't find him anywhere. He must be dead by now."

"And if he's dead, where is the body, Dieter? Where the hell is his rotting, skinny body? Where the hell? Have the rats eaten it? No! Rats don't eat other rats!"

19

That morning, when Olivier enters the room to give Marie Ann her breakfast and leave the tray on the bed, he finds the comedian has turned around. Instead of looking out of the window like he does every day, he is sitting with his back to the typewriter and his elbows on his knees, looking at Marie Ann on the bed. Next to the bed there are about one hundred pages neatly stacked, black on white. The black ink is becoming greyer by the day— "we don't have a replacement"—and this worries old Olivier. But he doesn't want to mention this to the comedian. He'll tell him when he finds the right moment.

Marie Ann lies with her eyes wide open, incapable of moving a single muscle. And the comedian stares at her.

"What happened?"

"A brain hemorrhages. She's been like that for three years."

A long silence follows.

"The worst is her expression. I doubt she would have chosen to keep that expression on her face for the rest of her life."

"Can she hear us?"

Olivier gives him a sad smile.

"What, you want her to listen to Wagner?" "Is she deaf then?"

"The doctors think so, but it's impossible to know. I prefer to think that she isn't. That when her time comes she will enter the next life with everything you have writ- ten in her head."

"It never crossed your mind to . . ."

"What, to kill her?"

"Yes."

"I'm an old man, these are different times . . . I'm from a different century . . ."

"I understand."

"How is the writing coming along?"

"It's coming along well. I think I'm almost finished."

"Can I read it?"

"I'd rather wait until it's all finished."

"We don't have any more ink."

"And no means of getting any more either, I guess?"

"It would be difficult . . . once the ink is finished, that's it."

"I think I'll manage . . . You know Olivier, I'm very grateful to you for not once calling me by my name."

"I, on the other hand, am very grateful to you for using mine."

"I don't know how all this is going to end, but thank you."

"I must thank you, you've lengthened my life. You've revived me."

"Here, I think I'm going to let you read it. I don't know if it's any good, but there you go."

"I'm sure it's good."

"I wouldn't be so sure."

The comedian leaves the room. Olivier starts to read. Slowly, a smile starts to form on his lips.

20

When the comedian left the house, Olivier and Marie Ann were asleep. Olivier had fallen asleep shortly after reading the last few lines of his manuscript, with an expression of complete peace and abandonment painted on his face and the hint of a smile on his lips. That smile was enough for the comedian to know the value of what he had written. The manuscript was good. He didn't want to hear opinions, praise or what the critics had to say. He didn't need those. That tranquil expression, the peace in Olivier's face and the almost-but-not-quite smile on his lips were enough. It seemed to the comedian, as he was leaving the room, that Marie Ann had opened an eye. But it was impossible: Olivier himself closed her eyes every night and opened them again come morning. He took the manuscript pages from the bed; he had to take the last one from between Olivier's fingertips, a quick tug did it. He placed the manuscript in a folder and headed for the street. The house couldn't have been any more than three hundred square feet in total. Apart from the room where Olivier and Marie Ann slept, there was a narrow kitchen, which he hadn't seen until then. He opened the door: he saw the little corner where Olivier must have slept, on the wooden rocking chair where a blanket lay. There wasn't even enough room to lie down on the floor. He looked at the rocking chair and the crumpled blanket before leaving; there was a coffee cup next to them. A shiver ran down his spine. It was unsettling how much the rocking chair looked like Olivier, it even had a hump. Objects can be merciless sometimes, they can steal the souls of the people who own them and embody them completely.

He said goodbye to the rocking chair, as if that substitute gesture could ease the guilt he felt at not being brave enough to say goodbye to Marie Ann and Olivier. It didn't work, and he reached the street feeling just as guilty.

Wearing a long raincoat belonging to Olivier, he went down the stairs. He found an unexpected present in one of the raincoat pockets: thirty dollars and a key that opened some unknown lock. He was going to need the money. As for the key, he decided to keep it as a good luck charm, knowing that it was unlikely to open the door to any place he knew.

After their triumphant first incursion the Nazis had relaxed somewhat, they didn't patrol the streets quite as fiercely. The gruesome punishments seen on the streets during the first few weeks were over; the bodies of members of the resistance were no longer hung from lamp posts as a warning and an example.

He found a room in the East Village.

"Ten dollars a week. And twenty more as a deposit."

The money hadn't lasted long. He gave the harpy behind the counter what she asked and she quickly made it disappear into her bra. She didn't ask for anything else apart from the money. Better that way.

It was a squalid tiny room that contained only a bed, a little table and a pitcher and bowl to freshen up. It took him a week to reread and correct the manuscript, and to fill in with black ink the increasingly pale gray marks the weak ribbon had left on the last few pages. He noted the advantages of small spaces during that time: he hardly needed to move to reach whatever place he wanted in that room. He could lift an arm from his bed, which he used as a desk, dip his hand in the pitcher and cool his tired eyes without having to get up from his chair. It was much easier to gather his thoughts and concentrate in that tiny room. Ideas have catlike tendencies: the more room they have, the more they meander. Living inside that small space was like living inside his own head. Moreover, he realized that, unconsciously, he pictured his brain to be something very much like the little room he inhabited.

It became a personal challenge, more than a game, his life in that tiny room. After a few days he had completely mastered a system of economy of movement that allowed him to do everything without leaving his bed: he could switch the radio on with his foot—only to switch it off immediately again, it was unbearable having Wagner on the radio all the time—and, with the other, he could roll the blind up and down. The only reason to move from his bed was a regular need to go to the bathroom.

As the days wore on he started to notice the smell of dampness in the room and to confuse it with his own body odor. It seemed to him that the wallpaper and his skin fulfilled the same purpose; that the wallpaper and his skin were the same thing, one thing, a synthesis of concrete and skin. He was comfortable there. He only went out once a week, to rummage rubbish bins for food when his hunger became unbearable. Once he found a boxing glove amid the rubbish. Its owner's hand was still inside it.

He couldn't stop throwing up all day. When he returned to the room his vision was blurred . . . it seemed to him that the wallpaper was exuding a yellow, bilious, repugnant substance.

After the second week he had to sing in the subway to pay his rent. It wasn't always easy: the Nazi patrols weren't very keen on *bel canto*. Even though he was fearful at the start, no one recognized him. He was dead and buried in the collective imagination: it didn't occur to anybody to say look, look how that clochard-homeless-good-for- noth-ing tramp looks like the comedian! Not one person. For a while he thought that it was painful to disappear from people's memories. It was painful at first, yes, but quite comforting after a while.

21

Eva. Eva. Eva.

Eva was asleep in his room. The little man pushed the covers back and stared at her naked body for a long while. He was looking for a signal. He wondered if the fact that he slept with a woman named Eva meant anything. Feeling suddenly paranoid, the little man numbered his ribs one by one: none missing, thank God. Eva, naked and shorn of her bedding, woke up with a shiver. She switched the light on.

"Why don't you come to bed, love?"

"Because I can't sleep. Don't be so stupid."

He was a man who made time yet never slept, he thought momentarily, but he chose not to follow that train of thought further.

Eva grabbed the sheets by a corner and, pulling away from the little man, buried her head under them.

The little man crossed the corridor toward the living room. There were a few dozen apples on a basket, shamelessly red against the muted, coffee-colored wallpaper. The little man flung the windows open. He saw that the sentry was asleep in his watch post. He took the basket and started throwing apples at him. The sentry woke up startled, hitting himself in the face with the shotgun in the process.

He would face the firing squad in the morning.

At the barracks, they ate apple compote for days.

22

The comedian often held the key he had found in Olivier's raincoat pocket in his hand. It was hard to fight the temptation to visit. But he couldn't do that. He had to move forward. Onward. Olivier and Marie Ann would understand it, he was sure. But lately he had been feeling exhausted, powerless, like he couldn't move forward or even take a step back. The manuscript had been finished for a while and he knew it was time for him to make decisions. He needed to find rehearsal space first, and after that, he needed to find actors to perform his theater play. It wasn't going to be easy.

He arrived at his guesthouse and paid the landlady the last week's rent. The chubby woman, no more than five feet tall, didn't ask any questions, not even of people who paid their rent in nickels and dimes.

He had no documents, nor the money to pay for a place to stay for any length of time. He heard of a guy in Chinatown called Kim who rented out wardrobes. He headed there, thinking that having a smaller place to live in would help him purify his mind and see everything more clearly; his ideas would be sharper, he would know the way forward.

For those used to cramped spaces Kim's wardrobes weren't so small. Kim told him the rules: no women, no dogs, and all of his clothes must fit on one hanger; that was easy, especially as he didn't have many spare clothes. It didn't bother him having his clothes swing above his nose every time an above-ground train went by, it almost felt like someone was with him. The wardrobe had two holes, one at either side, to allow for the circulation of air. He could sleep perfectly well inside it with his knees bent up. The wardrobe had these little rounded shelves in the corners: he piled up the half-empty tins of tuna and other edibles he found in rubbish bins on those shelves. He never let go of the manuscript inside the blue folder; every night he hugged it in his sleep. Inside the wardrobe, with the help of a candle, he kept reading and rereading the manuscript. His eyes were weaker and more tired every day. His vision was getting blurred. The lines were beginning to mount each other and blend together and undo each other; where there were once words and sentences, he started seeing lines of barbed wire; the fire, the explosions of battle and the craters it left behind, the destruction. Heat and more heat, unbearable heat. He woke up from the nightmare suddenly: one of the candles had set the trousers that hung above him on fire and the inside of the wardrobe was in flames. He grabbed the blue folder and jumped out in no time. Luckily the fire had spread upward, up his trousers, which were more flammable than any wood or coal, and more attractive to the flames than his prized manuscript.

Sadly, his wardrobe was completely consumed by the flames. Kim kicked him out without a second thought.

23

Ever since the little man had started eating bunches of grapes for breakfast Eva was worried.

"*An apple a day keeps the doctor away*. Didn't you ever hear that, love?"

Eva, Eva, Eva. Always Eva.

The advance guard was moving forward slowly but inexorably. On the map of the USA, the red string that linked the pins together kept moving westward, signaling the increasing swaths of conquered land. But the little man was getting bored, he was feeling isolated and alone in Manhattan. He often heard the pregnant women and the children screaming in the Woolworth building head- quarters. It was tiresome: especially when the soldiers— they too got bored—took the children from their mothers and, dangling them by the ankles out of a window, threatened them with the void in a will-I-won't-I-let-go game that frightened everyone sick.

On those nights when Eva buried her head under the sheets and slept so deeply, the little man started to go out for walks to try to shake off his insomnia, wearing a long plain raincoat so as not to be recognized. It was winter, the streets were empty; it was a lie that the city never slept.

His walks got longer every night, so much so he once ended up reaching the docks downtown. On the pier, he remembered fondly the grandiose German landing—a glorious day that seemed a distant memory now. But his joyful reminiscing didn't last long, as soon as his mind touched on the Marco Polo code and the comedian his memories took a bitter turn and everything that was good about that day disappeared. Only God knew where that son of a whore was. Maybe in California, working with the resistance. But it was hard to believe that they would keep such a well-known character in hiding. Maybe Dieter was right. Most likely he was dead by now.

24

The sudden loss of his living arrangements only brought urgency to a decision he had known for a while he would have to make. Being as he was used to living in small spaces, he could see what the next logical step was very clearly. Since his home was becoming more and more like a second skin, the next logical step was to contain his home within the confines of his raincoat, to reduce the size of his home just that little bit more. He didn't need a wardrobe anymore; if he stitched the lining of Olivier's raincoat strongly enough and compartmentalized the pockets cleverly, they could work as well as any shelves and store his tins and other goods. The decision was made: no sooner had he left his carbonized, tomblike wardrobe, then he knew he would live inside his raincoat. He went without food for a week to get a roof for his new home: he spent seven days' worth of food on a wide-brimmed hat. He hadn't allowed himself a treat like that in months. He held tight to the key in his pocket. His new home was ready.

He wasn't a clochard or a tramp, no. Perhaps it was hard at first sight to differentiate the comedian from one of them but he, unlike those tramps with lost eyes and uncertain fates, had a home, a very special one at that, one that he carried with him everywhere. As he did the blue folder, of course. From that night on, it became his pillow. And also, his table. There are many disadvantages to not having a home, no doubt, but there are advantages too: there is no need to ever sweep the floor, nothing ever gets lost in a remote corner, we lose no time wondering which room we'll be most comfortable in, and we never get unexpected visits from people we never invited over.

In the mornings he went to the subway to sing. In the evenings he walked up and down the city choosing always the less-patrolled streets, always carrying the manuscript inside its blue folder with him. Bit by bit he came closer to the Woolworth building, hoping to find out about the little man's movements. There was nothing he could do, of course. The building was completely secure. But something, an irrepressible force, brought him there all the same. As if by coming closer to his enemy he could increase his chances of defeating him one day. One day, a homeless woman approached him near the Woolworth building.

"Can I join you?"

"Do as you will."

"Want to know where to find good food?"

"I do well on my own, thanks."

"He's a proud one! You're new, aren't you? It's clear you're not from the streets."

The tramp's name was Kat. She must have been around sixty years old but some might have thought she was one hundred and twenty, except for her being so nimble. The circumference of her waist was not that different from a bourbon cask's, but she moved quickly all the same.

"Cigarette?"

He took one to be polite.

Kat lit her cigarette and the comedian's too. She pulled a face immediately and exhaled the smoke in disgust.

"*Shit!* Ever since the Germans got here even the tobacco has gotten worse."

The comedian said nothing. Kat was curious.

"You're too clean to be on the streets. Who are you? What are you carrying in that folder?"

"It's just something I wrote, it's not important."

"It's not important? You don't let go of it even when you sleep!"

"It's nothing important. I'm attached to it, that's all. It's very personal."

"Yeah right. You know what I think?"

"Whatever you're thinking is probably wrong."

"What I think is that you're carrying the money from last week's bank robbery there!"

The comedian laughed: he opened the folder and fluttered the pages in front of her, holding one corner of the stack with thumb and index. The sound the pages made was similar to the sound of money, but it was clear they were just pages, only that.

"Pity I can't read. Will you read it to me sometime?"

"Maybe. Maybe someday."

Didn't you need a squire? Thinks the comedian to him-self. Well, here is your squire, your Sancho Panza. Here, in the middle of this madness you're living through, in this world gone crazy, there she is, this clochard-homeless-good-for-nothing tramp whose entire worldly hopes and remaining glimmers of lost youth gather in her expectant eyes.

"And you, were you always on the streets?"

"Yes, always . . . ever since I ran away, at least."

"Where did you run away from?"

Kat rolled her eyes as far back into her skull as they would go—two white bowling balls rolling in parallel in the same direction—to signal that this was a secret that would remain well hidden deep under her eyelashes.

Her grey eyes doubted for a moment.

"Ever since the Germans got here even the tobacco has gotten worse, don't you think?"

A single bowling pin fell on the sidewalk, a skinny one, a cigarette, still burning.

25

Kat followed him everywhere. But the tramp didn't bother him at all, she didn't hold him back or annoy him, she was a good listener, a good friend, her voice was soothing. She didn't cast an uncomfortable shadow on his own shadow.

Once, when they were walking around the Lower East Side, the comedian stopped dead in his tracks to stare at Olivier's window. He had been wrong to leave as he did. He owed him a visit.

"I should go visit him, Kat."

"Who?"

The comedian held the key in his raincoat pocket tight.

"A friend."

"He can't be a very good friend: he's not exactly helping you at your hour of need, is he?"

Kat smiled. She had a few crooked teeth and, around them, a few blackened stumps buried in unhealthy gums.

"He doesn't know I'm living on the streets. He saved my life once."

"And he probably thought once was enough, right?"

"Wait here. I'll be back soon."

The comedian walks quickly toward Olivier's building.

Kat watches him go from where she stands. She shouts at him then, as if fearing he will leave for good, that she will never see him again.

"It was from the bug house!"

The comedian turns around. Kat's sharing of her secret is her means of binding him to her, not letting him go. I trust my pain to you so you won't leave me. I bare my soul to you so you hold it in your hands. That seems to be the deal.

"I've been living on the streets since the day I ran away from the bug house!"

The comedian gives her a reassuring nod, thanking her trust and letting her know he will be back soon, that she needn't worry. He enters Olivier's building with determination. His heart booms in his chest and his hands tremble when he knocks on the door. It occurs to him that the key in his pocket might be the key to that door, but he doesn't use it. Tremble, tremble, tremble . . . the word sounds like a badly shut door that rumbles in the wind in an abandoned cabin. Tremble. A wordsmith passed by and wrote it down in his notebook. Tremble. And ever since it's tremble. A good name for a word, the wordsmith made a good dictionary. He carries the blue folder under one arm, it is falling to pieces. The elastic doesn't travel down the same holes anymore, he had to pierce new ones. And it's full of knots too, the elastic, because it has broken in so many places. He has knocked on the door. Trembling. A ten-year-old boy with protruding ears opens the door. Immediately, his mother is at the door too. He was expecting an elderly gentleman.

"His name is Olivier."

"He died recently, the old man."

"Recently?"

"It's a sad story. They had to take the wife to a nursing home, she couldn't look after herself ... did you know them?"

"What about the rocking chair? Is it here still? Can I see it?"

"I'm sorry, we called the junk man and he took it away ..."

Tremble.

"Was it important?"

The comedian turns around without a word. Mute cinema. Olivier is dead, dead under his hump. Dead on his rocking chair, his shell. And Marie Ann trapped in a home, agonizing, unable to escape.

He pressed the cold key hard in his palm. If only he could give her this key, at least.

Kat is waiting for him outside. She is teasing a dog with a torn boxing glove. The comedian remembers the boxing glove he found once, with its owner's hand still inside. Was this its companion glove? Maybe the island of Manhattan is just the body of a buried boxer. Either way the dog is happy, it barks and jumps excitedly—the torn boxing glove is a great prize.

"How did it go? No luck, right? Look here, I found us a new friend."

26

Olivier's last thought.

He is on a boat and the boat sways gently on the sea, the waves are small, they sing a beautiful cadenza, like a soothing lullaby, soft and sweet. He opens one eye and realizes that there is no boat, that he is sitting on the rocking chair, at home, in the kitchen. Somehow, he fell asleep. He extends an arm, he wants to reach the doorknob with- out getting up. He holds the doorknob tightly. He is still sitting down. His arm is at a familiar angle, it forms a nice hollow, perfect for him to put his head on it. He lets his head fall between the curve of his arm and his downward-pointing elbow. He smiles.

When the men arrive from the morgue, Olivier's hand is still holding firm to the doorknob. So much so, a carpenter has to come over and saw the doorknob off the door. And so, they bury Olivier Legrand like that, door- knob in hand, in a cemetery on Staten Island that over- looks the statue of the lady who extends a hand toward the sky.

Does the doorknob open any doors where you are, Olivier?

Did you open the door to Manu and the others, his two kids who, not long after leaving their mother's breast, bled to death in the trenches of the Great War? Maybe the key in the comedian's pocket could be of use to you now? Are there drifts for you to dig and fill up where you are?

If the answer is yes, send light to our windows. A bit of light, enough to make a knife's blade or a hair comb glint in the sunlight. Maybe we'll be able to ride that light and get the hell away from here.

"It was a bughouse! I've been living on the streets since the day I ran away from the bughouse!"

27

Leaving Eva in bed, the little man walks down to the docks again in the middle of the night. He watches a dog play with a torn boxing glove. Then he notices the fat hand that holds the boxing glove. It belongs to an old woman sheltering among cardboard boxes on a street corner, whose waist is not that different from a bourbon cask's. She is one of those good-for-nothing tramps who don't respect the curfew. And lying next to her, a man who can't sleep, his head resting on a blue pillow and his wide-open eyes staring at the night sky, wearing a raincoat similar to his. He must be very cold, he's trembling. He raises himself a little, scratches his head and musses up his dirty hair. He rubs his arms up and down and takes the pillow in his hands. It's a blue folder. The little man stares at the folder. And the hand that holds the folder. The hand with missing nails, and the arm that follows that hand. And up the forearm, past the elbow, one shoulder and then the other, and between them a neck. And on top of that neck, a face he can't stop staring at. The little man gulps in disbelief. He is overwhelmed; he can't very well tell if it's by disgust or by ire. Ire wins when the little man comes to the conclusion that the man in front of his eyes is the comedian.

"You! *Wiener! Kraut! Schnitzel!*"

28

From the distance, you can just about see something moving in the shadows. Kat, tired of playing with the dog, has fallen asleep, and at first can't see a thing. Afterward she can, but it is all happening too far away for her to be able to do anything about it. The comedian and the little man are fighting on the pier. Darkness reigns. The comedian or the little man, one of the two, runs toward the bridge and is followed by the little man or the comedian, one of the two. The one running ahead must be the comedian, since he's carrying the blue folder under one arm. Or maybe for that very reason it's the little man, who has stolen the blue folder from the comedian and wants to destroy it. One leaps toward the other, they are like two school kids playing at recess. But this is no kids' game. Bashing his face hard against the port's cobbled streets, one man breaks the other man's teeth, and the blood makes patterns like crosses as it spreads between the gaps. One man slides his hand into a pocket and takes a key out, the key falls to the ground. They scramble for it. One-man grabs hold of it and sticks the cold metal into the other man's eye, and as if the eye were a lock, gives the key a turn, opening God knows what.

They are far away, we don't know who's the one screaming, covering a bleeding eye with his hand. We can't even
hear the screams: it is silent cinema.

One man runs away screaming, the other one chases
him—screaming. It looks like the second one is the comedian, because he is wearing a wide-brimmed hat—the roof
of his house—and carries the blue folder under one arm,
the folder with the broken elastic, which contains the manuscript. The manuscript written by the window in Olivier
and Marie Ann's home. The comedian and the little man
are fighting to the death. The man whose eye has been used as
a lock knows he has lost his eye. It is amazing how he won't
give up despite that, how he keeps fighting.

Now they are near the water, on the empty piers: they
roll around on the ground several times, almost falling in
the murky waters. The man carrying the blue folder runs
up the steps of the Brooklyn Bridge. But the man running
behind him is not wearing a hat anymore. Who is who,
then, at this point?

Now the fight is on the bridge. One man presses the
other against the railing, the folder falls to the ground, a
cold, icy gust of wind opens it. Pages start to fly out of
it, slowly at first, but soon they gather courage and float
freely, rampant, like nude flesh out of a constraining corset.
Nude white flesh first branded in gray by an Under-wood
typewriter, then written over with black ink, flies free in the
wind up to the sky and into the river. Kat sees the white
pages float in the black night like white kites. She scrunches
up her tired eyes hoping to read something on them, forget-
ting that she can't read. One of the two men tries to rescue
some pages, but it's all in vain. One of the two—we don't
know which—is pressed against the railing, the other gives

him a push and he falls into the water without vaulting over, without spreading his arms; a dead weight, defeated, resigned to his fate. The man still on the bridge stares at the one who is falling. Does he look with one eye or with two? There is no way of telling.

And the manuscript is lost in the river asdfgh qwerty.

29

The following morning, we are still hopeful. We hope against all hope that when dawn breaks, each and every window of the city will be plastered with a page of the manuscript. Maybe we can will it so. Come dawn, the manuscript that was written looking out of a window in the city will return to the windows of the city, and its citizens will read it there, the light will tell them what to hold on to, what to do; in the end, the manuscript was written looking at them, somehow, they had a part in the writing of it too. It was their mirror, the window they shared. In it they will see age and recognize scars, and then, then they will flock to the streets. It is a possibility, it might hap- pen yet, although it isn't certain that it will. The window panes still look leaden.

The East River always promenades its drowned, but today the promenade takes place underwater; an underwater parade. It is almost impossible to witness such a peculiar parade, so different from the military ones that take place above, on the cobbled streets; it can only be seen by those who pay very close attention. One of the men parading underwater jumps upward: you can see his hat guiding the current. Because down there, people can walk underwater: you can see the air bubbles surfacing while there are no lights on the windows yet.

If you see a hat being carried by the current, it is a sign that someone is walking underwater.

And if there is no hat on the water, it is a sign that the hat-wearer is holding on to the railing and walking up or down the stairs.

An old dog won't let go of Kat's glove. Then Kat opens the palm of her hand and, even though there is nothing there, even though Lady Liberty's crown isn't there, even though that void isn't a drift from which some precious mineral has been extracted, the dog shoves its snout into the palm of Kat's hand. It isn't clear if it's always the same dog that shoves its snout into Kat's open palm. It isn't clear if it is even the same hand. Kat tries to remember something between glugs. Something that doesn't belong to her, maybe even something she has never thought. She lies back on the grass in Central Park and caresses her cheek with a blade of grass, trying to capture the elusive memory. But she doesn't. Sinking deeper into the grassy earth she smiles and rejoices in the fact that the long grass hides the skyscrapers from view.

A bark is all that's needed; time collapses. The screen cracks, the celluloid is torn apart. The projector keeps rolling. A synagogue, a child playing with sawdust. Someone called Brevesky.

Different strata. Layers. Grass softly drying on haylofts high above, creeping grass spreading up the statue of a hunchbacked hero.

The hamlet of Braunau, in Germany, is covered in snow, one day around the turn of the twentieth century. Someone is using an umbrella as a crutch and pushing the overgrowth aside; an umbrella to pierce the snow and the centuries, seeking to reach new strata.

Typewriters gather dust in pawn shops. There are things inside things and little worlds inside bigger worlds, bound together with fine twine. People file their nails in offices, roadsides, tunnels, intending to dig holes in coal mines and other solid matters. The newspapers are packed tight and bound with hemp rope, and the headlines are still invisible.

A new day is about to start. There are no lights in the windows yet. The carpenter marks the wood with his pencil—something must reach this far, who knows what—places the pencil behind his ear and starts sandpapering the staircase's handrail. Swoosh. Swoosh. As the air fills with particles of sawdust, the surface knots in the wood disappear and other knots and other eyes, buried deep in the wood, emerge. Even though the carpenter has plied his trade for a long time, those eyes in the wood still surprise him. As soon as he tries to make one disappear, another one appears, another dark, staring pupil. The smell of freshly shorn sawdust is everywhere. Swoosh. Swoosh. He gives the handrail one last pass with the sandpaper and decides it is ready.

"What do you say, Mr. Brevesky?"

Mr. Brevesky looks down and nods.

(Paris, December 2002—Donostia, October 2004)
(Translated into English in New York, 2010)

Amaia Gabantxo is a literary translator, writer and critic and her work has been published the United States, the United Kingdom, Spain and Ireland. She has translated novels, short stories and poetry by authors such as Bernardo Atxaga, Miren Agur Meabe, Anjel Lertundi, Lourdes Onederra, Unai Elorriaga, Kirmen Uribe, Harkaitz Cano, and most other prominent writers in Basque. She has received many grants and awards for her work, and regularly takes part in conferences and literary events worldwide. She moonlights as a flamenco singer.